KT-394-109

CONTENTS

Some of the projects in this book require the use of needles, pins and safety pins.
We would advise that young children are supervised by a responsible adult.

A FAIRYTALE DRESS

Woodland fairies live in a secret world of their own. They wear clothes made from leaves and flowers.

Making a costume can be messy work! Make sure you cover all surfaces with newspaper before you start.

Make a forest fairy outfit using:

A vest or t-shirt

A bin liner (preferably green)

Coloured plastic bags (preferably green, yellow and orange)

100-cm length of green ribbon

Sticky tape

A pair of scissors

A needle and thread

A ruler

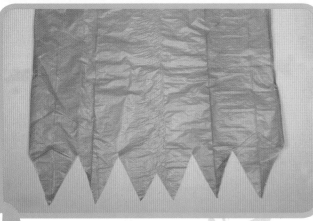

1 Cut the bin liner to the length that you want your skirt to be. Cut triangles out of the bottom edge.

2 Ask an adult to help you cut two slits in the middle at the top of the bag. The slits should be about 4 cm apart and 2 cm from the top of the bag. Pull the ends of the ribbon through the slits that you have made. The ribbon ends should be inside the bag.

3 Fold the top edge of the bag over so that the ribbon is hidden and the ends are now outside the bag. Stick tape along the edge to hold in it place.

Dressing up as a
FAIRY

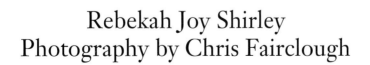

Rebekah Joy Shirley
Photography by Chris Fairclough

W
FRANKLIN WATTS
LONDON SYDNEY

12696640

This paperback edition printed in 2012 by Franklin Watts

Copyright © 2011 Arcturus Publishing Limited

Franklin Watts
338 Euston Road
London NW1 3BH

Franklin Watts Australia
Level 17/207 Kent Street, Sydney, NSW 2000

Produced by Arcturus Publishing Limited,
26/27 Bickels Yard, 151–153 Bermondsey Street, London SE1 3HA

The right of Rebekah Joy Shirley to be identified as the author of this work has been
asserted by her in accordance with the Copyright, Designs and Patents Act 1988.

All rights reserved.

Series Concept: Discovery Books Ltd., 2 College Street,
Ludlow, Shropshire, SY8 1AN
www.discoverybooks.net
Managing editor for Discovery Books: Laura Durman
Editor: Rebecca Hunter
Designer: Blink Media
Photography: Chris Fairclough

The author and photographer would like to acknowledge the following for their help in preparing this book:
the staff and pupils of Chad Vale Primary School, Jack Coady, Iqrah Choudhury, Ayla-Belma Hadzovic,
Sunny Marko-Bennett, Abbie Sangha.

A CIP catalogue record for this book is available from the British Library.

Dewey Decimal Classification Number: 646.4'78

ISBN 978 1 4451 1401 9

Printed in China

Franklin Watts is a division of Hachette Children's Books, an Hachette UK company.
www.hachette.co.uk

Supplier 03, Date 0312, Print Run 1797

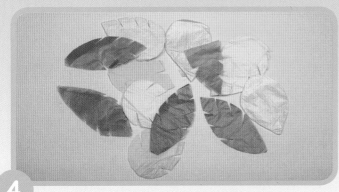

4 Cut leaf shapes out of different coloured carrier bags.

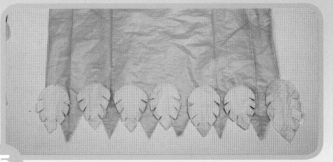

5 Using sticky tape, fix a row of leaf shapes at the bottom of the bin liner.

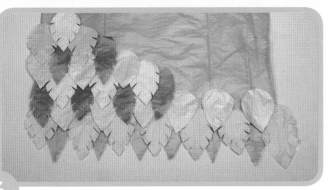

6 Stick another row of leaves above the first row, **overlapping** it slightly. Continue adding rows until the bag is covered.

7 Sew the leaf shapes onto your t-shirt or vest. Sew two stitches at the top of each leaf.

Carefully put on your fairy top. Then tie the ribbon around your waist to wear your skirt. You're ready to play in the forest!

FLUTTERING WINGS

Fairies fly using their beautiful, sparkly wings. Fairy wings are very **fragile** and must be handled with care.

To make your own wings you will need:
Four metal coat hangers
A pair of coloured tights
Sticky tape
15 tinsel pipe cleaners
Polystyrene balls
Craft glue and a paintbrush
6 metres of sequin ribbon
A pair of scissors
100-cm length of elastic

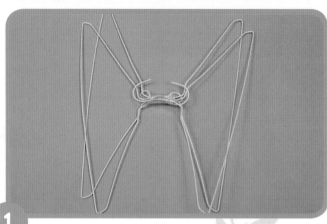

1 Take two coat hangers and join them at the twisted part by the hooks. Use sticky tape to secure. Then attach the other two coat hangers on top of them in the same way.

2 Cut the top off the pair of tights. Cut each leg in half.

3 Stretch these four pieces over the wire wing-shapes and tie at the back. Ask an adult to straighten the hooks.

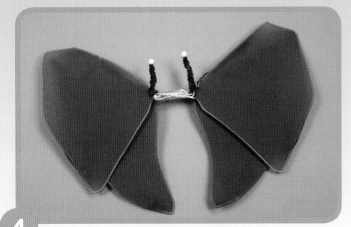

4 Glue **polystyrene** balls to the end of each straightened hook and wrap tinsel pipe cleaners around them.

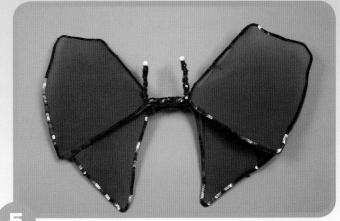

5 Glue sequin ribbon around the edges of the wings and to cover the joined area in the middle.

Put your arms through the elastic loops and flutter away with your fairy friends!

6 Glue tinsel pipe cleaners onto the wings in curly patterns and shapes.

7 Cut two 50-cm lengths of elastic. Tie them to the middle of the wings to make two loops.

FAIRY FEET

Fairies wear beautiful, **dainty** shoes on their feet so that they can skip silently through the forest.

Make your own fairy slippers using:
Fun foam
A hole punch
Ten lengths of ribbon, each about 50 cm long, in three or four different colours
A pair of scissors
A ruler

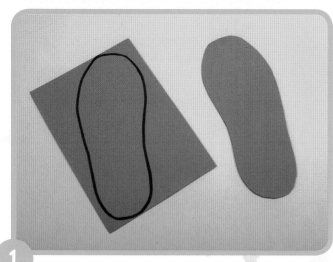

1 Draw around a pair of your shoes on a piece of fun foam. Then cut the shapes out.

TIP:
If the foam is too thick to use a hole punch, ask an adult to make the holes in the foam for you.

3 Punch four holes towards the back of each shoe as shown above.

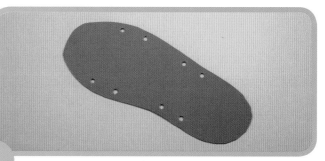

2 Punch four holes at the front of each shoe as shown in the picture. The holes should be about 2 cm apart and 1 cm from the edge.

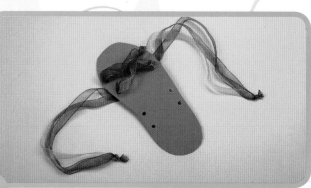

4 Thread three of the ribbons through the front holes. Thread them in a criss-cross pattern.

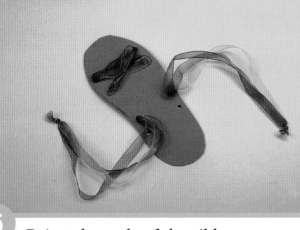

5 Bring the ends of the ribbons up through the front two holes at the back of each shoe. Tie a knot at each end of the ribbons.

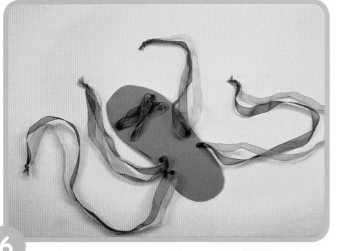

6 Take two more ribbons and thread them through the two holes at the very back of each shoe. Then tie a knot at the ends.

Tie the ribbons in a criss-cross way finishing with a bow at the back of your leg. Now you are ready to skip through the forest in your fantastic fairy footwear.

FLOWERS FOR A FAIRY

Fairies love to gather flowers from the forests and meadows. Make this bunch of flowers and little ladybird to impress your fairy friends.

To make your own flowers you will need:
Coloured tissue paper
Green pipe cleaners
A pair of scissors
Red and black felt
Two plastic eyes
Craft glue and a paintbrush
A ruler

1 Cut the tissue paper into rectangles about 6 cm by 16 cm.

TIP:
For smaller flowers make smaller rectangles.

2 Fold each piece of tissue paper backwards and forwards down the length of the paper until the whole rectangle is folded up. Then tie one end of a pipe cleaner around the middle.

3 Trim the ends of the tissue paper strip. You could cut the end into a point or a rounded shape.

4 Gently spread out the paper folds on both sides to make a flower shape. Repeat to make a whole **bouquet**.

Glue the ladybird onto a flower. Carry your beautiful flowers with you wherever you go. You could also use them to decorate your hair, clothing and shoes.

5
Cut out a circle of red felt about 3 cm in diameter. Also cut out an oval of black felt and four small circles.

6
Glue them all to the red circle.

7
Glue two plastic eyes to the ladybird.

A 'MAKE-A-WISH' WAND

Fairies carry a magic wand with them wherever they go. They use the wand to **grant** wishes.

Make your own wand using:
A ruler
A pen or pencil
Card
Metallic foiled paper
Craft glue and a paintbrush
Sequins
Craft gems
30-cm length of 10 mm dowel
1-metre length of ribbon
Sticky tape
A pair of scissors

1 Fold a piece of card in half. Use a ruler to draw half a star onto the card along the fold.

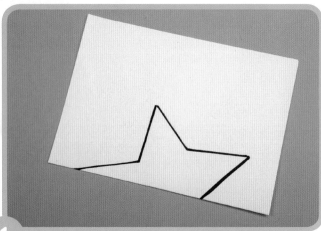

2 Cut out the shape and unfold the star. Then draw a smaller star in the same way.

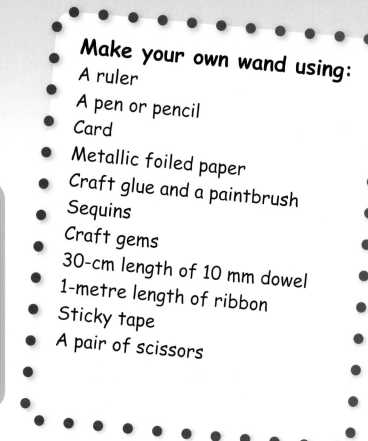

3 Draw around the star shapes on metallic foiled paper. Cut the shapes out.

4 Glue the metallic paper onto the card stars and glue the stars together. Decorate with craft gems and sequins.

5 Glue one end of the ribbon to the bottom of the dowel. Wrap the ribbon around the dowel and tape it at the end.

6 Use strong sticky tape to attach the dowel to the back of the star.

Now wave your wand and make someone's dream come true. Whose wish will you grant first?

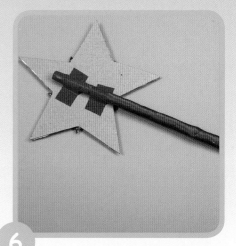

A HEAVENLY HEADBAND

Woodland fairies wear beautiful headbands made of forest **vines**, leaves and flowers.

Make your own forest headband using:
- Green pipe cleaners
- Coloured paper or plastic
- Craft glue and a paintbrush
- Coloured tissue paper
- A pair of scissors

1 Make a crown as the base of your headband by wrapping ten pipe cleaners around each other to form a circle. The circle needs to fit comfortably on your head.

2 Cut leaf shapes out of coloured paper or plastic.

3 Make some small paper flowers in the same way as you did on page 10.

4 Twist the pipe cleaners to add the flowers to your headband. Then glue the leaves to the headband.

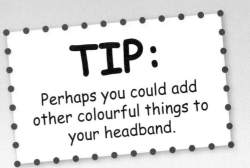

TIP:

Perhaps you could add other colourful things to your headband.

With your headband in place you will look like a fairy queen with a tiara!

JOLLY JEWELLERY

Fairies always look beautiful. They wear jewellery made from forest treasures around their necks, hands and feet.

Make a bracelet and necklace using:
String, wool and ribbon
Thread
Pipe cleaners
Craft feathers

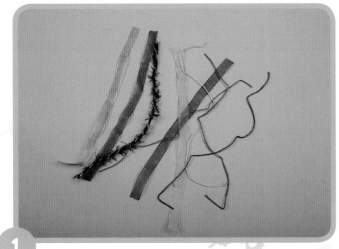

1 Cut several lengths of string, wool, ribbon and thread long enough to fit around your wrist.

2 Twist the lengths together around a pipe cleaner and tie in place. Tie on some feathers using thread.

3 Twist the ends of the pipe cleaner together to make the bracelet. You can alter it to make it fit your wrist.

You can make several bracelets in different colours. Tie some around your ankles. Now you are ready to frolic in the forest with your fairy friends!

4 Cut six 1-metre lengths of string, wool, ribbon and thread.

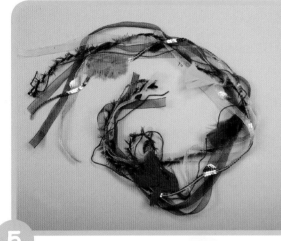

5 Twist the lengths together, adding feathers as before. Leave two long ribbons for tying.

6 Tie the ends of the necklace in a bow.

A FLUTTERING FRIEND

Fairies make friends easily with the **creatures** that surround them. They particularly love playing with the beautiful butterflies that flutter through the forest.

Make your own butterfly companion using:
9 tinsel pipe cleaners
A pair of scissors
Metallic card
Craft gems
Glitter glue
Sticky tape
A ruler
Craft glue and a paintbrush

1 Take two pipe cleaners and wrap the ends around your finger a couple of times to make the **antennae** of your butterfly.

2 Use six pipe cleaners for the body of the butterfly. Join these to the antennae by wrapping another pipe cleaner around them. The antennae should stick out at the front.

3 Pull two of the pipe cleaners in the bundle out to one side. Wrap the ends back around the body to make loops for wings.

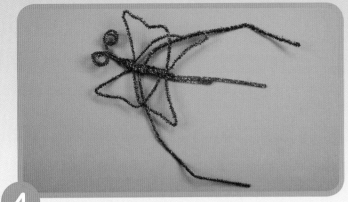

4 Repeat to make two wing shapes on the other side. Then pull another pipe cleaner out on each side and leave them loose.

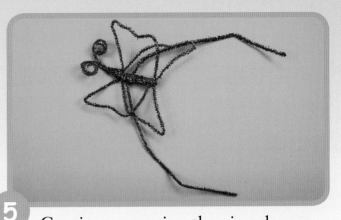

5 Continue wrapping the pipe cleaner from step 2 around the body until it is about 10 cm long. Cut off the end.

Use the two loose pipe cleaners to attach the butterfly to your arm. What a beautiful fairy friend!

6 Cut out four wing shapes from metallic card and decorate them with glitter glue and craft gems.

7 Use sticky tape to attach the card wings to the pipe cleaner loops.

FAIRY DUST

Fairies use **enchanting** sparkles and dust to spread magic. They carry the fairy dust around in a special pouch.

Make your own fairy dust pouch using:
- An old sock
- Ribbon
- A wool needle
- A pair of scissors
- Sequins
- A ruler

1 Cut the toe end off an old sock so you are left with a pouch about 15 cm long.

2 Thread the ribbon onto a large wool needle. Weave it in and out of the top edge of sock. You can use the two loose ends later to close the pouch.

3 Cut three 50-cm lengths of ribbon. Plait the ribbons together. Then repeat with another three 50-cm lengths of ribbon.

4 Tie one of the plaits through a ribbon loop on the left-hand side of the pouch. Tie the other plait through a loop on the right-hand side.

5 Fill the pouch with sequins.

Tie the plaited ribbons around your waist. Now you can sprinkle magical fairy dust whenever it is needed!

A FAIRY'S BEST FRIEND

Some of the fairies' best friends are the elves that live in the forest. Elves are very **mischievous** and love to play games and have fun.

To make an elf costume you will need:
A green t-shirt
A pair of scissors
A tape measure
Brown felt
Green felt
Craft glue and a paintbrush
A jingle bell (or pompom)

1 Cut triangles out of the bottom of the t-shirt. Cut triangles along the sleeve edges, too.

TIP:
You could follow the instructions for the fairy dress to cover your elf t-shirt in leaves if you like.

2 Measure around your waist with a tape measure. Cut a strip of brown felt that is 4 cm wide and 20 cm longer than your waist measurement.

3 Cut out a circle of brown felt about 50 cm across. Cut triangles around the edge.

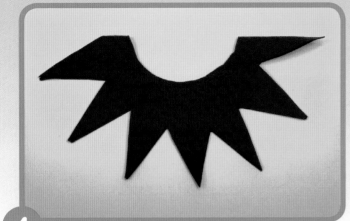

4 Fold the circle in half and cut a small semicircle out of the middle through both layers.

5 Cut a quarter circle with a **radius** of about 30 cm, out of green felt. Glue the edges together to make a cone shaped hat.

TIP:

If you don't have a jingle bell, you could glue a pompom to the top of the hat instead.

6 Glue or sew a jingle bell to the top of the hat.

Become an elf by putting on the t-shirt, collar and belt. Then pop your hat on your head. Pull it down on one side to give your outfit an impish look!

GLOSSARY

antennae the long, thin 'feelers' on an insect's head
bouquet a bunch of flowers
creature an animal
dainty delicate and pretty
enchanting magical
fragile delicate and easily broken
grant to give something as a favour
mischievous playful and naughty
overlap to put part of one thing on top of another
polystyrene a white, foam-like material
radius the measurement between the centre of a circle and its edge
vine a plant that creeps and twists its way through other plants

FURTHER INFORMATION

The Complete Book of the Flower Fairies by Cicely Mary Barker (Warne, 2010)
50 Fairy Things to Make & Do by Rebecca Gilpin and Minna Lacey (Usborne Books, 2009)
A Field Guide to Fairies by Susannah Marriot (Kingfisher, 2009)
The Fairyspotter's Guide by Meg Clibbon (Evans Brothers, 2006)

www.flowerfairies.com/home.html
The official website of Cicely Barker's classic Flower Fairies.
www.cottingleyconnect.org.uk/fairies.htm
Learn about the extraordinary story of the Cottingley Fairies.
www.disney.co.uk/DisneyOnline/fairies/
The official Disney Fairies website. Meet fairy friends, play games and take part in activities.

INDEX